NOW, NOW, FRIENDS! LET'S NOT QUARREL.

O HOLY ONE, YOU TELL US. WHO DID YOU REALLY BLESS?

I··· ER··· I BLESSED THE MOST FOOLISH AMONG YOU.

AH, THERE! WHAT DID I TELL YOU? I WAS THE ONE.

WHO SAYS SO? I AM THE GREATER FOOL. HE BLESSED ME!

WAIT. ALL MEN ARE FOOLISH. THEREFORE I HAVE BLESSED ALL OF YOU.

O MAHATMA, NEVER HAVE WE HEARD SUCH WORDS OF WISDOM.

SUCH GREAT WORDS CAN COME ONLY FROM A GREAT MAN.

WE WILL FOLLOW YOU AND LISTEN TO YOUR WORDS OF WISDOM.

THUS, OVERNIGHT, PARAMARTHA, THE SIMPLETON, BECAME GURU PARAMARTHA. HE NAMED HIS FIVE FOOLISH DISCIPLES, MADDI, MADHAYA, MILECHA, MOODHA AND PEDDA. AND SINCE ALL GURUS AND THEIR DISCIPLES LIVE IN ASHRAMS, THE SIX OF THEM BUILT ONE AND STARTED LIVING IN IT.

ONE DAY, THE GURU AND HIS DISCIPLES SET OUT FOR A TEMPLE IN A NEIGHBOURING VILLAGE. ON THE WAY—

O LEARNED GURU, WHAT IS LIFE?

IT'S SO SIMPLE. LIFE IS WHAT ALL LIVING THINGS HAVE.

AND ALL LIVING THINGS MOVE.

NOW, LOOK AT THIS TREE. ITS LEAVES MOVE. IT'S A LIVING THING.

OH, GREAT GURU, YOU EXPLAIN THE MOST DIFFICULT THINGS IN THE MOST SIMPLE WAY!

WE ARE FORTUNATE TO BE YOUR DISCIPLES.

LATER IN THE EVENING, THE GURU AND HIS DISCIPLES HAD TO CROSS A RIVER.

IS THIS RIVER A LIVING THING?

OF COURSE, CAN'T YOU SEE IT MOVING?

IT MOVES. EVER SO LITTLE, BUT IT MOVES.

WOULD IT BE ANGRY IF WE CROSSED IT?

WE MUST CROSS IT ONLY WHEN IT'S ASLEEP.

THEN I'LL GO AND SEE WHETHER IT'S ASLEEP.

WE'LL WAIT HERE FOR YOU.

I'LL PROD IT WITH MY TORCH.

LATER, ON THE OPPOSITE BANK—

AT LAST! MADHAYA, SEE IF ALL OF US ARE HERE.

MADHAYA STARTED COUNTING.

ONE, GURU···

···TWO, MOODHA···

···THREE, PEDDA···

···FOUR, MILECHA····

···FIVE, MADDI···

HEY! ONE OF US IS MISSING!

IT CAN'T BE! LET ME COUNT.

PARAMARTHA LIKE MADHAVA, COUNTED EVERYONE EXCEPT HIMSELF.

ALAS, MY DEAR BOYS! THE RIVER HAS TAKEN ITS TOLL. WE HAVE LOST HIM, HE WON'T COME BACK.

WHY ARE YOU WAILING, MY FRIENDS? WHAT'S THE MATTER?

WE WERE SIX. WE ARE ONLY FIVE NOW.

YES, WE WERE SIX. THE RIVER CLAIMED ONE OF US.

FOOLS! BUT WAIT... I CAN PROFIT BY THEIR FOOLISHNESS.

YOU ARE LUCKY, MY FRIENDS. I AM A MAGICIAN. I CAN BRING BACK YOUR FRIEND. BUT WHAT WILL YOU GIVE ME IN RETURN?

9

THAT WAS AN EXCELLENT BARGAIN. NOW LET US REST FOR A WHILE.

WE'VE GOT THE EGG. BUT WHO WILL HATCH IT?

ONE OF US WILL HAVE TO DO IT, OF COURSE.

EACH ONE OF THE LAZY DISCIPLES HAD HIS OWN EXCUSE.

I HAVE NO TIME. I'M ALWAYS BUSY WITH PREPARATIONS FOR THE POOJA.

I AND MADDI HAVE THE GARDEN AND THE GROCERY TO ATTEND TO.

I AM BUSY THE WHOLE DAY COOKING FOR ALL OF US...

... AND I HAVE TO ATTEND TO THE GUESTS.

DON'T WORRY, MY BOYS. I AM ALWAYS FREE. I WILL HATCH IT.

IF THE EGG IS HATCHED BY YOU, O MAHATMA, A FINE HORSE IS SURE TO COME OUT.

GURU PARAMARTHA AND HIS DISCIPLES TOOK LEAVE OF THE 'EGG-SELLER'.

IT WAS A REAL PIECE OF LUCK THAT WE SAW THOSE EGGS.

IT'S ALL GOD'S WORK. HE KNEW HOW MUCH I LONGED FOR A HORSE.

AS THEY TRUDGED ON—

OOOH! HELP! OW! THE EGG!

OH, NO! IT'S BROKEN!

JUST THEN A FRIGHTENED RABBIT RAN OUT OF ITS HOLE NEAR THE FALLEN PUMPKIN.

WHAT'S THAT... LOOK!

IT'S THE BABY HORSE! DON'T LET IT GET AWAY!

WHERE HAS IT GONE? WE MUST FIND IT. WE'LL GO THIS WAY. YOU GO THAT WAY. QUICK!

LATER—

IT'S NOT HERE!

IT'S NOT HERE EITHER. LET'S GO BACK TO THE OTHERS.

I THINK WE'VE LOST IT AFTER ALL. WHAT A SHAME!

O GURU, PLEASE DON'T BE CROSS WITH US. THE LITTLE HORSE WAS TOO QUICK FOR US.

NEVER MIND, MY DEAR BOYS. IT'S ALL FOR THE BEST. YOU'VE JUST SAVED MY LIFE!

CAN YOU IMAGINE WHAT WOULD HAPPEN IF I HAD TO RIDE THAT HORSE?

YOU WOULD BE THROWN OFF AND GET KILLED!

OH, NO! THANK GOD, WE LOST THE HORSE!

YES. THANK HIM WITH ALL YOUR HEART AND SOUL.

AND THE GURU AND HIS DISCIPLES CONTINUED THEIR JOURNEY.

AS THE DAY GREW WARMER—

PHEW! I AM DYING OF THIRST.

I'LL GET YOU SOME WATER.

THE DISCIPLE RAN TO A POND NEAR BY TO FETCH THE WATER.

WHEN THE STRANGE FISHING-TACKLE WAS READY—

AS LUCK WOULD HAVE IT, THE END OF THE SICKLE GOT ENTANGLED IN A BUNCH OF WEEDS.

A FEW DAYS LATER, GURU PARAMARTHA AND HIS DISCIPLES WERE DISCUSSING A MATTER OF GREAT IMPORTANCE.

WE HAVE HARDLY ANY FUNDS LEFT.

PEOPLE HERE ARE VERY MISERLY. THEY BRING US NEITHER GIFTS NOR MONEY.

WE CAN'T SIT HERE AND WAIT FOR THEM TO COME AND DONATE GIFTS. WE MUST GO TO THEM.

AS YOU COMMAND, O GURU.

SO NEXT MORNING, GURU PARAMARTHA AND HIS DISCIPLES SET OUT ON A FUND-RAISING TOUR.

ON THE WAY, THE GURU'S TURBAN SLIPPED FROM HIS HEAD AND FELL.

WHAT A NUISANCE! ONE OF THEM IS SURE TO PICK IT UP.

AFTER A LITTLE WHILE—

PHEW! IT'S HOT. WHERE IS MY TURBAN?

IT MUST BE FAR BEHIND US NOW.

FOOLS! DIDN'T YOU HAVE THE SENSE TO PICK IT UP?

FORGIVE US, GURU. I'LL RUN BACK AND PICK IT UP.

THEN GO. AND IN FUTURE PICK UP ANYTHING THAT'S DROPPED ON THE WAY AND GIVE IT TO ME.

THE TURBAN WAS SOON RESTORED TO THE GURU AND THE GROUP WALKED ON.

AFTER THEY HAD COVERED SOME DISTANCE, THE GURU'S HORSE DROPPED SOME DUNG.

QUICK! PICK IT UP.

THE HORSE DROPPED THIS ON THE WAY.

GOD HELP ME! NOW ISN'T THIS THE LIMIT!

WHY ARE YOU CROSS WITH ME?

24

YOU ASKED US TO PICK UP WHATEVER WAS DROPPED AND I OBEYED YOU.

IF WE DON'T PICK UP WHAT IS DROPPED, OUR GURU IS CROSS. IF WE DO, HE'S CROSS. I'M UTTERLY CONFUSED. HOW ARE WE TO SERVE HIM?

DON'T WORRY. YOU'LL LEARN BY EXPERIENCE AND I AM ALWAYS THERE TO GUIDE YOU.

PERHAPS IF YOU GIVE US A LIST OF ALL THE THINGS WHICH HAVE TO BE PICKED UP, WE COULD SERVE YOU BETTER.

GURU PARAMARTHA MADE THE LIST AND GAVE IT TO HIS DISCIPLES.

SEE THAT YOU FOLLOW IT STRICTLY. GO BY THE RULE. ALWAYS.

DON'T WORRY GURU. RULES ARE RULES AND WE WILL NEVER BREAK THEM.

AS THEY WENT FURTHER ALONG THE ROUGH ROAD, THE HORSE STUMBLED.

MADDI, MOODHA, PEDDA... HOLD ME! HOLD ME, SOMEONE!

AT LAST GURU PARAMARTHA WAS PULLED OUT OF THE DITCH AND TAKEN BACK TO THE ASHRAM.

AH! IT ALL COMES BACK TO ME NOW!

THAT BRAHMANA'S PREDICTION YEARS AGO... THAT MY END WOULD BE BROUGHT ABOUT BY WATER...

LEAVE ME ALONE, DEAR BOYS. I MUST WAIT FOR MY END.

THE DISCIPLES OBEYED HIM AND GAVE HIM NEITHER FOOD NOR WATER TILL ONE DAY HE COLLAPSED.

I THINK THE END HAS COME.

HE IS ONE WITH GOD NOW.

BOO-HOO-HOO! OUR GURU HAS LEFT US! WE ARE ORPHANED!

HUSH! FRIENDS! THIS IS NOT THE TIME TO CRY. ARRANGEMENTS HAVE TO BE MADE FOR THE LAST RITES.

Available on the iPad!

A chemical engineer by profession, Anant Pai gave up his job to follow his dream, a dream that led to the birth of Amar Chitra Katha and Tinkle.

Anant Pai - Master Storyteller traces the story of the man who left behind a legacy of learning and laughter for children. ACK Media's new iPad app brings alive a new reading experience using panel-by-panel view technology, created in-house.